Dragonsitter
Trick or Treat?

First published in 2016 by
Andersen Press Limited
20 Vauxhall Bridge Road
London SW1V 2SA
www.andersenpress.co.uk

2 4 6 8 10 9 7 5 3 1

British Library Cataloguing in Publication Data available.

ISBN 978 1 78344 459 5

Printed and bound in Great Britain by
Clays Limited, Bungay, Suffolk, NR35 1ED

The Dragonsitter:
Trick or Treat?

Josh Lacey

Illustrated by Garry Parsons

Andersen Press
London

Dear Uncle Morton

Can I borrow your dragons?

Next week there is a Fancy Dress Competition at the Halloween Parade.

The first prize is a new computer, which is exactly what we need.

Our computer is Dad's old one. He left it behind when he moved out, and that was four years ago, and it was already ancient then.

Also Emily spilt a glass of milk on the keyboard and now the keys only work if you press them really hard.

All our problems would be solved if we won that prize.

1

Unfortunately we don't have very good costumes.

I was planning to go as Frankenstein's Monster, but I can't find any bolts for my neck.

Emily wants to be a ghost, but that just means wearing a sheet and going "Whoooo, whoooo" and she's never going to win anything for that.

Could we borrow your dragons?

With them we'd be sure to win first prize.

We would only actually need Ziggy and Arthur for one night, but Mum says you are welcome to stay for the whole week, as long as you don't mind sleeping on the sofa.

Granny is staying for half-term, and I bet she would really like to see you too.

Love from

your favourite nephew

Eddie

From: Morton Pickle

To: Edward Smith-Pickle

Date: Wednesday 25 October

Subject: Re: Halloween

 Attachments: I ♥ Oregon

Dear Eddie

I would have loved to join you for Halloween. There are few things that I like more than tricks and treats. Sadly though I must stay here in Scotland, because I am hard at work preparing for my trip to Oregon in search of Bigfoot.

However, Gordon has kindly volunteered to come in my place. I think he just wants an excuse to see your mother. He is always complaining about how much he misses her.

As you will see for yourself, Arthur is going through a growth spurt at the moment, and hasn't quite mastered the art of breathing fire. You may want to keep an extinguisher handy.

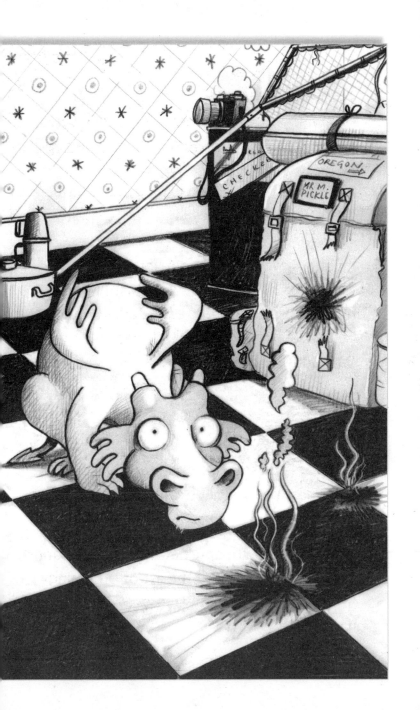

Thank you for the picture of your costumes. You both look lovely, but I can see why you need a little help. I'm sure the dragons will be just the job. If they aren't, perhaps you could persuade your mother to buy you a new computer? Or a second-hand one? Surely they aren't too expensive these days.

What a pity that I shall not get to see my own mother. But please do send her my best wishes.

With love from

your affectionate uncle

Morton

Dear Uncle Morton

Thank you very much for sending the dragons with Gordon.

I promise we will take very good care of them.

I know we've had a few disasters before, but this time will be different.

I just hope we win first prize. The computer isn't going to live much longer. It keeps moaning and groaning, and the screen has gone wobbly.

I asked Mum if she could buy us a new one, but she said single-parent families can't afford luxuries like brand-new computers.

She said even a second-hand one would be too much for us in the current economic climate.

I asked what the current economic climate was, and she said gloomy.

Love from

Eddie

Dear Uncle Morton

Do you like our tam-o'-shanters?

Gordon gave them to me and Emily. He says we look like proper wee Scots.

He also brought lots of presents for Mum.

We just ate some of the smoked salmon with our scrambled eggs.

Mum said it was the most delicious breakfast of her entire life, and I think it might have been mine too.

I see what you mean about Arthur breathing fire. He's already had a few accidents. But Mum said it didn't matter.

I think she's just pleased to see Gordon.

Also he had a pee on the carpet. (Arthur, I mean, not Gordon.) But you can't blame him for that. He must have been desperate after driving all the way from Scotland.

When everyone has recovered, we're going to make our costumes.

I've changed my mind about Frankenstein's Monster. I'm going to be an Egyptian mummy instead.

Emily is still planning to go as a ghost, and the dragons can just be themselves.

I'll send you lots of pictures.

Love from

Eddie

From: Edward Smith-Pickle
To: Morton Pickle
Date: Saturday 28 October
Subject: HELP!!!!!!!!

 Attachments: The proposal

Dear Uncle Morton

We have a big problem and we need your help.

This afternoon Gordon asked Mum to marry him.

Obviously that's not the problem. We all really like Gordon. Especially Mum.

The problem is he got down on one knee and pulled a ring from his pocket.

Then he said, "Will you marry me?"

Mum literally couldn't speak.

If only she had said "yes" straightaway.

Then Gordon could have put the ring on her finger and everything would have been fine.

Unfortunately Mum just stood there with her mouth open, staring at the ring as if she'd never seen anything like it before.

Which gave Arthur enough time to fly across the room and snatch it out of Gordon's hand.

I don't know why he did that. I've never eaten a ring myself, but I can't imagine they're very tasty.

Even so he swallowed it quicker than you could say "I do".

Mum and Gordon tried to force Arthur's mouth open and pull the ring straight out again, which wasn't exactly sensible.

Gordon is very upset. Not just about his burnt fingers, but also about the ring.

It belonged to his great-aunt Isla. She wore it every day for sixty-seven years.

Now it's inside Arthur's tummy and we don't know how to get it out.

Do you have any brilliant ideas?

Love from

Eddie

From: Morton Pickle

To: Edward Smith-Pickle

Date: Saturday 28 October

Subject: Re: HELP!!!!!!!!

Attachments: A wee dram

Dear Eddie

I'm terribly sorry to hear about Gordon's great-aunt's ring.

Unfortunately I can't imagine any way to extract it from Arthur's stomachs. (As you will remember from reading my book, dragons have three.)

If I were you, I would simply keep Arthur indoors for the next couple of days. The ring is sure to progress steadily through his guts and emerge eventually in his poos. Make sure you check them thoroughly. Once you have washed the ring, it will be as good as new, if not even better.

To speed up the process, you could feed him some dried fruit. Figs or apricots would be perfect.

Don't forget to keep all your doors and windows firmly closed. All would be lost if Arthur was allowed to leave the house and take flight. You would never find the ring again if he did a poo in mid-air.

On a quite different subject, please convey my congratulations to Gordon and your mother.

I hope they don't mind, but I have already announced the good news to Gordon's uncle, Mr McDougall. Tonight we drank a wee dram together in celebration.

Is Gordon planning to move south? Or are you all going to come and live in Scotland? I hope you do. I couldn't imagine having nicer neighbours than you and Emily.

With love from

your affectionate uncle

Morton

From: Edward Smith-Pickle
To: Morton Pickle
Date: Saturday 28 October
Subject: The oven
 Attachments: Our tea

Dear Uncle Morton

I asked Mum if we were moving to Scotland or staying here, and she said she hasn't had a moment to think about the wedding, let alone where we're going to live.

Mostly she's been worrying about how to get the ring out of Arthur.

She said she was going to kill him. I am almost sure she was joking. Even so, I locked him in the oven.

He didn't seem to mind. He just curled up and went to sleep.

I think he must have known it was for his own safety.

I would have liked to keep him in there
till he had a poo, but we're having jacket
potatoes for tea.

Mum said turning the oven on would be fine, Arthur or no Arthur, but Gordon wasn't sure that was such a good idea.

I don't think he was too concerned about Arthur's personal safety. He just thought Arthur might explode, taking the ring with him.

So now he's in a cardboard box on the kitchen floor.

Love from

Eddie

Dear Uncle Morton

Mum says we can't go to the Halloween Parade unless we get the ring out of Arthur.

I asked why not, and she said we have to understand that actions have consequences.

I said that's not fair, because it wasn't me and Emily who swallowed the ring, but she said that's not the point.

I asked what was the point, and she said I should think about it.

I have been thinking about it. A lot. But I still don't know.

All I do know is this: if we are going to win that new computer, we have to get the ring out of Arthur.

Do you have any other ideas apart from apricots and figs?

I've been feeding him them both, but they don't seem to be having any effect.

He just won't poo.

What can we do, Uncle Morton?

We need that computer. We really do.

The screen on this one is flickering so much it's given me a headache.

Also the space bar fell off. I strapped it back on with Sellotape, but I don't know how much longer it will last.

Love from

Eddie

Dear Uncle Morton

Today Arthur ate a packet of apricots and a packet of figs plus six sausages and two lamb chops, but nothing came out the other end.

Granny said cod liver oil would get things moving.

We had some in the bathroom cupboard, so I tried to give a teaspoon to Arthur, but he wouldn't touch it.

Granny says hello by the way. She arrived from Spain this morning.

She wants to know why you never go and visit her.

I said you were very busy with Bigfoot and the Yeti and your dragons, and she said what kind of son is too busy to visit his own mother, Bigfeet or no Bigfeet.

Also she wants to know when you're going to settle down and have some children of your own?

She thinks you should take a leaf out of Mum's book.

I told her you have the dragons instead, but she said they don't count.

Love from

Eddie

Dear Uncle Morton

The Fancy Dress Competition is tomorrow night. Our costumes are finished. Mine looks brilliant, and so does Emily's. I bet we'd win first prize.

But Arthur still hasn't had a poo, so we're not even going.

I can't understand why he won't. I've fed him about a hundred figs and apricots. Also he had three toffee apples.

Mum spent the afternoon making them. She said she needed something to take her mind off the ring.

I only ate half of mine. It wasn't very nice. But Arthur gulped down three of them without even blinking.

Granny said we should hold him upside down and shake him till the ring comes out.

I explained about Arthur's new fire-breathing abilities, and Granny said she wasn't scared of a few flames.

I said even so it probably wasn't a good idea, but she took no notice.

I really don't know why Granny got so cross about her new shoes. If you fed me two packets of figs and three toffee apples, then held me upside down and shook me, I would probably be sick too.

Granny says if you had a scrap of decency you would come down here yourself and clear up this whole mess.

I don't know whether she means the sick or the swallowed ring.

Maybe she means both.

But do you think you could do that, Uncle Morton? Couldn't you just come here and sort things out?

We really do need some help.

Eddie

From: Morton Pickle
To: Edward Smith–Pickle
Date: Monday 30 October
Subject: Re: Toffee apples

Dear Eddie

I'm terribly sorry, but I simply don't have time to come south and help you. You wouldn't believe how many books have been written about Bigfoot, and I am hoping to read them all before I leave.

At the same time, I am cleaning and checking every inch of my camping equipment. Yesterday I found a big hole burnt through the middle of my tent. Arthur must have had another accident while I wasn't looking. I spent the entire evening sewing it up with a square of new canvas and some thick thread.

I am terribly sorry that he is proving so obstinate. I can only suggest that you try massaging his stomachs. Perhaps you can ease things towards the exit.

I hope the ring emerges in time for the competition, and you manage to win first prize. I shall be thinking of you tomorrow night.

What a pity that I shall not get to see my mother. Please send her my best wishes. I shall make every effort to visit her in Spain as soon as I can.

With love from

your affectionate uncle

Morton

From: Edward Smith-Pickle

To: Morton Pickle

Date: Tuesday 31 October

Subject: Costume changes

 Attachments: Mummy; Devil; Witch

Dear Uncle Morton

I wish I could say Happy Halloween, but it's really not.

There are only a few hours till the start of the Fancy Dress Competition, but Arthur still hasn't had a poo.

I don't know why we even bothered trying on our costumes.

I did what you suggested and massaged his tummy, but he didn't like that one bit. In fact he blew a big blast of fire directly at me.

Gordon says my Egyptian mummy costume looks even more authentic with a bit of smoke damage, but I know he's just trying to be nice.

Luckily I've got a skeleton costume upstairs in my cupboard, so I'm going to change into that.

Gordon's costume is amazing. I never would have thought he could look like the devil, but he really does. He even has horns on his head and a forked tail which swings from side to side when he walks.

Granny looks quite frightening too,
although she's just wearing a witch's hat
made from a cereal packet.

Even Emily is a bit scary in her sheet.

It's a pity no one is going to see us.

Eddie

From: Edward Smith–Pickle

To: Morton Pickle

Date: Tuesday 31 October

Subject: Zombie attack

 Attachments: Toffee apples; Zombie rampage

Dear Uncle Morton

The Fancy Dress Competition starts in one hour, but we're still at home.

Gordon suggested we try apple bobbing. Apparently that's traditional in Scotland on Halloween.

But I don't feel like bobbing apples.

I want to win first prize in the Fancy Dress Competition.

By the way, your dragons haven't just ruined Halloween for us. They've now messed it up for several other people too, because only ten minutes ago, the doorbell rang. I grabbed the tray of toffee apples and opened the front door.

There were three zombies outside waving their arms and shouting "Trick or treat! Trick or treat!"

They were dripping blood all over the front garden.

They looked very realistic.

In fact, Ziggy must have thought they were actually zombies, because she shoved me aside and breathed a great gust of orange fire at them.

Then she chased them down the garden path.

I've never seen zombies run so fast.

If Ziggy carries on like this, we're going to have a lot of toffee apples left over.

Eddie

From: Edward Smith-Pickle

To: Morton Pickle

Date: Tuesday 31 October

Subject: Trick or treat?

Attachments: Neighbours; Parade; Sugar rush; Fireworks

Dear Uncle Morton

Happy Halloween!

This time I really mean it.

Mum let us go to the Halloween Parade.

Gordon persuaded her to change her mind. I don't know how he did it, but they were whispering for ages, and then she said yes.

I think she must be in a good mood because of getting married.

Granny said let's see if it lasts.

I asked if she meant the good mood or the marriage, and Granny said, "Either would be nice."

Anyway Mum said we could go Trick or Treating and enter the Fancy Dress Competition as long as we behaved ourselves, and didn't talk to strangers, and looked both ways before crossing the road, and always did exactly what Granny and Gordon said.

Mum stayed behind with Arthur, just in case he pooed, so only five of us went: Emily the ghost, Granny the witch, Gordon the devil, me the skeleton, and Ziggy as herself.

First we went Trick or Treating.

Gordon let us ring the bell of any house with a pumpkin in the window.

You wouldn't believe how many sweets we got.

Every house was just the same. We hardly even got a chance to say "Trick or treat?" People took one look at Ziggy and handed over whatever they had.

Gordon said we had enough to open a sweet shop.

I know you don't like Ziggy having too many sweets, so I only gave her a few.

Even so she got a bit of a sugar rush. Her eyes went a bit wild and her whiskers started twitching.

I didn't give her any more after that, but unfortunately Emily handed over a bunch of lollipops and two whole packets of gummy bears.

Ziggy gulped them down without even bothering to take off the wrappers.

Then we went to the high street for the Halloween Parade and the Fancy Dress Competition.

The high street was jam-packed with ghosts and ghouls and vampires and witches and wizards and trolls and goblins, plus two Batmans, three Robins, and a princess, although I don't know what she was doing there, since princesses aren't exactly Halloweeny.

We all marched past the judges. They were taking notes on all the costumes and whispering to one another.

What happened next was probably my fault.

I was trying to look really skeletony in front of the judges, so I wasn't taking very much notice of Ziggy.

I don't know if I could have done anything even if I had been taking notice of her, but at least I could have tried.

The first thing I heard was a loud hiccup.

Then she did an enormous burp.

When I turned to look at her, she was flapping her wings.

I tried to grab her, but it was already too late.

She flew straight up into the air, and did a somersault.

Then she did about seventeen more while breathing fire in every direction.

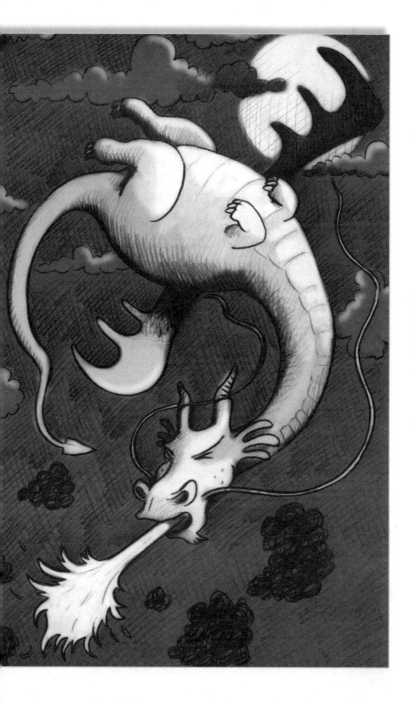

Everyone was cheering and clapping.

It was like our own personal firework display.

The judges were watching her too. They were all pointing into the sky and looking completely amazed. I hope they didn't forget to look at our costumes.

I wanted to go back and walk in front of them a second time, but Granny said it was time to go home.

She's used to Spain, so she feels the cold more than the rest of us. She says it gets into her bones.

I hope you're having a good Halloween in Scotland. Did you get any Trick or Treaters on your island?

Love from

Eddie

From: Edward Smith-Pickle

To: Morton Pickle

Date: Wednesday 1 November

Subject: Space bar

Attachments: Fatty

Dear Uncle Morton

I hope you can read this, because there is a fizzing sound coming from the back of the computer and I don't know how much longer it will even work.

Also the space bar fell off again and now I'm using half a pencil instead.

Gordon says I get full marks for ingenuity, but first prize in the Fancy Dress Competition would be even better. I just hope the judges got a proper look at our costumes.

They are announcing the prizes tomorrow, so we are all keeping our fingers crossed.

Arthur still hasn't had a poo. His tummy is getting so big he can hardly even fly any more. I'm really quite worried about what will happen if he doesn't poo soon.

Do you think dragons can explode?

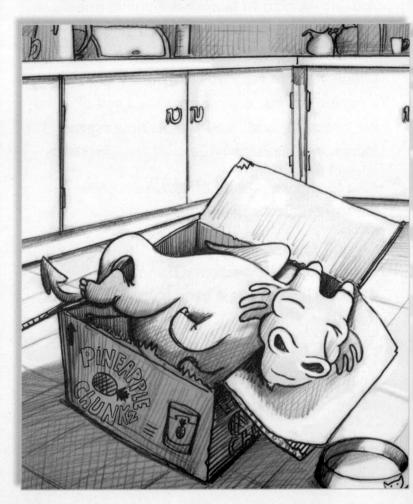

Mum says he has to stay in his cardboard box just in case.

She doesn't want bits of him all over her kitchen.

You will be glad to hear that Ziggy is fine after her sugar rush. She has spent the whole day asleep.

We haven't given her any more sweets.

We haven't actually had any more ourselves. Mum confiscated the whole lot and put them in the cupboard.

We're going to be allowed one a day on weekdays and two on Saturdays and Sundays.

At that rate they'll last us till next Christmas.

Love from

Eddie

From: Edward Smith-Pickle

To: Morton Pickle

Date: Thursday 2 November

Subject: Thief

📎 **Attachments:** The cupboard

Dear Uncle Morton

We didn't win the competition.

We did get a prize, but it wasn't first.

Gordon says third prize is just as good as first, but I know he's only trying to be nice.

Also a bunch of flowers really isn't as good as a new computer.

Mum says we'll have to wait till she gets a pay rise.

I just hope she gets one soon. The noises coming out of this computer are getting stranger all the time.

Also you owe me some sweets.

Actually Ziggy and Arthur do, but Mum says you're their owner, so any thefts or breakages are your responsibility.

This morning before anyone came down for breakfast your dragons broke into the cupboard.

I don't know how they got in there. The latch on the door is too hard for me to open. But somehow they managed to twist it round.

They took all my sweets, and all of Emily's too, and some others which Mum was keeping for a special occasion.

To be honest we're quite annoyed with them.

I wouldn't have minded giving them a few of my sweets, but why did they have to eat them all?

Granny says you were always stealing sweets from the cupboard when you were a little boy.

I couldn't imagine you stealing anything from anywhere, but Granny said you used to be a little terror.

Did you really, Uncle Morton?

Love from

Eddie

PS Click this link to see the whole story:
http//www.bestlocalnews.co.uk/vampire-wins-first-prize.html

COUNTY NEWS UPDATE:
Vampire Wins First Prize in Halloween Parade

This year more than two hundred people attended the traditional Halloween Parade.

During the evening, they were lucky enough to see a surprise firework display provided by a local resident.

The Fancy Dress Competition was judged by a panel of local experts, who said the standard was higher than ever.

After a long and heated discussion, the judges awarded first prize to a vampire.

Agnes Kranowski, 11, was dressed as the daughter of Count Dracula, while her brother Tomas went as her coffin.

Agnes and Tomas went home with a brand-new laptop from the Technology Store, the perfect place to upgrade your computer and purchase any accessories.

Second prize of £50 of books from The Village Bookstore went to Michelle Hussein, 7, who was dressed as a headless ghost.

Third Prize of £10 of flowers from Betty's Blooms went to a skeleton and his magnificent Chinese dragon kite.

The winner of the third prize has not yet come forward to claim their flowers. If you are the owner of the skeleton costume and the kite, please contact Betty at Betty's Blooms.

Dear Uncle Morton

Arthur has pooed out the ring!

It must have been the sweets that did it.

When we came down for breakfast there was an enormous steaming black poo on the carpet near the back door.

On top of the poo was the ring.

It looked like the cherry on a cake.

Unfortunately it isn't really a ring any more. It's more like a lump.

The gold must have melted while it was inside Arthur.

The diamond is fine. It came unstuck from the rest of the ring, but it's perfectly clean now we've washed off all the poo.

Unfortunately Mum can't wear the diamond on her finger without its ring.

Gordon is very upset. He says his great-aunt Isla would be turning in her grave if she could see it.

Emily said rings don't really matter and what's important is getting married to the person you love.

Gordon said his great-aunt Isla wouldn't think so.

I hope he isn't having second thoughts.

Love from

Eddie

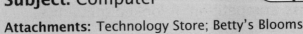

From: Edward Smith-Pickle

To: Morton Pickle

Date: Saturday 4 November

Subject: Computer

Attachments: Technology Store; Betty's Blooms

Dear Uncle Morton

I am writing this on OUR NEW COMPUTER!

Can you tell?

It's amazing being able to see the screen.

Also all the keys on the keyboard work.
Even the space bar.

Gordon bought it for us.

Actually, he didn't really buy it for *us*.
He bought it for Mum, so she can do her
spreadsheets for the wedding.

But Mum says Emily and I can use it
whenever we want, as long as we're not
playing games or wasting time.

We got it this afternoon from the Technology Store. While we were there I saw the computer which was first prize in the Fancy Dress Competition. It looked quite nice, but ours is even better.

After the computer shop we went to Betty's Blooms to collect our prize.

Betty wanted to know why we hadn't brought our Chinese kite to the shop. I explained she was asleep.

She wanted to know where she could get one of her own, and I said she would have to find the right cave in Outer Mongolia.

Also she wrote down the name of your book. She's going to get it out of the library.

Then Betty gave us the £10 token and we bought a big bunch of flowers.

They were really pretty.

In fact Gordon thought they were so pretty he bought them from us for £20.

I said that was much too much, but he said it was money well spent.

He gave £10 to me, and £10 to Emily, and the flowers to Mum.

I've got to go now. Mum and Gordon want to use the new computer to plan their wedding.

We've been helping them decide the menu.

They're going to have a ceilidh.

I thought that was something to eat, but actually it's a kind of Scottish dance.

Gordon has been teaching us how to do it.

Love from

Eddie

PS Mum says would you be able to give her away?

From: Morton Pickle
To: Edward Smith-Pickle
Date: Saturday 4 November
Subject: Re: Computer

Dear Eddie

Congratulations on your new computer!

I'm terribly sorry that Arthur ate all your sweets. Of course I shall buy you and Emily many more when we next meet.

I certainly didn't steal any sweets myself when I was a boy. My mother must have mixed me up with someone else.

Please tell your own mother that I should be flattered to give her away at her wedding. When will it be? I shall put the date in my diary and make sure that I am in the country.

You will be glad to hear that my preparations for Oregon have gone swimmingly and I shall be setting out on the trail of Bigfoot just before Christmas. Would you like to come too?

With love from

your affectionate uncle

Morton

Dear Uncle Morton

I hope you're going to be at home today, because Ziggy and Arthur are on their way back to Scotland.

Gordon left first thing this morning. If he doesn't hit any bad traffic, they should be back in time for tea.

Mum is still feeling a bit weepy.

They haven't decided the date of the wedding, but Mum says you will be the first to know.

I said shouldn't me and Emily be the first to know, and Mum said it was just an expression. So maybe you will be the third to know.

I'd better go now. We're taking Granny to the airport. She's flying back to Spain.

She is very sorry she didn't get to see you, but at least she met your dragons.

Love from

Eddie

PS I asked Mum if I could go to America with you to search for Bigfoot, and she said only when I'm 18. Could you wait till then?

The Dragonsitter's Island

Josh Lacey
Illustrated by Garry Parsons

Dear Uncle Morton,
The McDougalls are here. Mr McDougall won't stop shouting
and waving his arms. He has lost three sheep in a week.
Now he wants to take your dragons away and lock them in his
barn till the police arrive.

Eddie is dragonsitting on Uncle Morton's Scottish island.
But something is eating the local sheep.
Can Eddie find the real culprit?

Praise for *The Dragonsitter*:
'Ideal for young readers,
and belly-busting laughter
for all the family'
We Love This Book

9781783440450 £4.99

The Dragonsitter's Party

Josh Lacey

Illustrated by Garry Parsons

Dear Uncle Morton

Can you come to my birthday party? It's going to be great.
We're having a magician. Mum says your dragons aren't
invited, but you can take some cake home for them.

It's Eddie's birthday and he's looking forward to a
birthday party filled with fun, games and . . . dragons?
Ziggy and Arthur are the unexpected guests, but their
idea of a good time involves eating everything in sight
and ruining the party magician's tricks.
Is Eddie in for the wrong kind of
birthday surprise?

Praise for *The Dragonsitter*:
'Josh Lacey's comic timing
is impeccable'
Books for Keeps

9781783442294   £4.99

The Dragonsitter
to the
Rescue

Josh Lacey
Illustrated by Garry Parsons

Dear Uncle Morton

I have to tell you some bad news. We have lost one of your dragons. He's somewhere in London, but I don't know where.

Sightseeing is the last thing on Eddie's mind when the dragons escape on a trip to London. Will he find them before they get into hot water?

Praise for *The Dragonsitter*:
'Will entertain any child of 7+'
The Times

9781783443291   £4.99